I0547713

Friends Again

Friends Again

by Fiorentina

ProPress Books, Inc.
Massapequa, New York

ProPress Books, Inc.
Massapequa, New York
http://www.propressbooks.net

ISBN 978-0984519736
PRINTED IN THE UNITED STATES OF AMERICA

Dedicated to all of my best friends, from the twins in California to the twins in New York. ☺

Acknowledgements

Ahh, the acknowledgements. This is the part of the book I was really dreading to write. So many people to thank and so little space. I'll try and squeeze you all in.

First of all, a big thank you to my grandmother, grandfather, and to my parents for supporting me completely in my decision to design and draw the cover of this book myself. Same goes for the entire writing process. I love you all and thank you.

Thank you to Lee for pushing me to do things I don't want to do, whether it be talking in public or saying a simple "hello" to someone I don't know. You've helped me a lot in the past three years, so thanks *(a lot)* for everything.

A giant thanks to Michael and Kyle for being the awesomely annoying brothers I've grown to love. Sure they're loud, hyper and slightly smelly, but life wouldn't be the same without them. Love those dudes.

A big ol' thank you to two of my cousins, Lauren and Dana, for just being awesome. We've spent a lot of time annoying Grandma, separately and together. Let's keep up the good work.

And, last but not least, thanks to all of my friends: Sophie, Lilly T., Lilly W., Carly, Gianna, Ashley, Steve, Kailee, Jordan, Chloe M., Vicki, Chloe Y., Corrine, Alexa, Haylee, and Amanda. You are the greatest friends anyone could ever ask for. You're all amazingly awesome in your own special ways, and I know that even when we fight, we'll always be "Friends Again."

I'm such a dork. ☺

Chapter One

I LIKED HAVING A FRIEND LIKE Stevie. She was a good person, a nice one. With her spiky orange hair and her bright green eyes, she reminded me of a fairy. Except for the fact that she was a walking encyclopedia and knew the name of every city in America, North and South, she was a great friend. Which was why when she nagged and annoyed me, I usually let it slide. Usually.

"I'm bored," she complained one day, with her glasses falling off her nose. She adjusted them slowly and cleared her throat, shivering because of the cold. We sat in my tiny cottage of a house, testing lipgloss colors on our wrists and eye shadow on our eyelids. I ignored her and focused on my painting. I ran the eye shadow brush over my closed eyelid, struggling not to giggle at my scrunched up face. I pretended not to hear her and let her continue her nagging.

"Bored, bored, bored."

"Yeah," I replied, "I got that."

"I mean, there's nothing to do here! The only good thing at your house is your mother's makeup, and the one time she lets us use it, you're making pig faces in the mirror!"

I giggled. "I'm not making pig faces. I'm *painting.*"

She threw a pillow at me. "Don't be a goof. I'm just saying that maybe we could...I don't know...go *outside* for once?"

"Nope," I said coolly, "I like it in here. There are dogs outside. With fleas. And fur. And did I mention the fleas?"

Stevie rolled her eyes at me. Again her glasses fell. They were too big. She didn't bother to adjust them as she replied, "I haven't fainted in three years, Tina. I'm so over that stupid fear." She tugged at the blanket I sat on, causing me to drop the brush and put my hands up in defeat. "I want to... go... outside!"

"Fine," I jokingly-but-not-really-snapped, "but if we see any dogs out there, I am so not protecting you from them."

She rolled her eyes again. "If we see any dogs out there, I won't need protecting." She pulled me up, grabbed my arm, and dragged me to her cousin Garrison's house on the other side of town.

That's why I never went outside.

"Hey Tina," Garrison had said three months earlier, flashing me and Stevie one of his famous million-dollar smiles. Because of his dimples and shockingly sea-blue eyes, the girls around us swooned. He sat in the seat we'd saved him and grinned.

3

He cleared his throat. Stevie and I turned to him.

"Hey Stevie," he said. After she said "hey" back, we expected his grin to subside. It never did.

"Okay, I can't take it anymore," Stevie cried after a few moments of grinning silence. She looked at her cousin and exclaimed, "You look like The Joker. *What* are you so happy about?"

Garrison grinned still, but this time, he spoke at the same time. "I was going to tell you some good news, but now…"

"Tell me," I said, always up for something good. Garrison's grin finally disappeared, but only because he was being sarcastic. He made a big point of leaning closer to me, whispering in my ear, and flickering his eyes to Stevie, who pretended not to be annoyed. But the joke was on her. He hadn't said anything.

He turned back to Stevie and said, "Don't you just want to know?"

"Come on, Garrison. Haven't we had enough?" I shook him by the shoulders and said, "Tell us!"

Garrison's eyes smiled, but his mouth stayed in a thin pink line as he suppressed the grin forming on his cheeks. His eyes darted around us as he whispered, as if he were scared someone would hear, "I made the basketball team."

"What?"

"I made the basketball team."

"What?"

He rolled his eyes and shouted loud enough for the whole bus to hear, "I made the basketball team!"

Stevie and I widened our eyes. "No way!" we shrieked. Being on the basketball team was the highest honor in the history of our school, Winthrop Junior High. Sports were very important to us, the most competitive school in all of New Jersey. If he actually had made the team and did a good job, he would be worshipped.

Garrison would be popular. And if he was popular… *we'd* be popular.

"I am so joining the girl's team!" I cried, pumping my first in the air. Since the boys' tryouts were earlier, they'd all picked their sports. The girls had a longer time to choose. But there was no hesitating now.

Stevie's head snapped to me, "But we were going to do cheerleading!" I raised my eyebrows at how innocent she sounded, almost as angelic as a three-year-old girl.

"We were?" I asked, looking and feeling pretty surprised. "Since when?"

"Since forever," she said, crossing her arms and tapping her foot. "I distinctly remember…" Just then the bus slowed to a stop, the doors creaked open and interrupted my now-angry friend. In walked the oh-so-perfect Michael DeCaprio and his new best friend, Genevieve Williams.

Michael was gorgeous. He had short, chin-length black hair that fell, no matter how it was styled, perfectly beside his cheeks with his bangs falling in his eyes. His skin was annoyingly pretty and tan because of the many days he spent in the sun, and was flawless, even with his elf-like ears. Stevie and I always joked that they became so large from the earrings he wore. His ears were pierced when he was ten. (At least, that was the rumor going around.)

His eyelashes were long and curled, as if a massive coat of mascara had been applied... which they probably had been, even though he was a boy. Michael was a ninth grader, but in our school, which was an old-fashioned junior high, he acted much, much older. My mom always told me that I was very mature for my age, but the way Michael acted, not to mention dressed, implied that he knew how old he seemed and used it to his advantage. He was the coolest and scariest boy who ever lived.

That's when the Williams girl walked up to us. "Hey guys," she said, flipping her average-length, wavy blonde hair. With her tan skin, green eyes, freckles, and hint of an Australian accent, she was the stereotypical Aussie girl. She smiled at all of us as if we were old friends sharing a good joke. Which we *so* weren't.

The bus stopped for the last time. Kids in the front waddled lazily out the door, but since we sat in the back, we had a few extra minutes of stalling before going into the school.

"So," Miss Williams started, "I heard about you making the basketball team. You're so lucky." She played with her longer blonde hair and smiled, showing us her dimples. I raised my eyebrows, wondering who she was talking to.

Garrison seemed to be thinking the

same thing. He paused for a moment, his mouth hanging open, searching for the right words. The only thing he could utter was, "Me?"

She laughed. It was a silent one, where her shoulders shook and her mouth moved, but no sound came out. I was thankful.

Michael joined in on this mysterious laughter. His laugh was loud and annoying, but no one seemed to realize. His only flaw. If only someone noticed it.

After a minute of laughing, we could finally see the bus aisle. We could've left then, but we didn't.

Finally, after this awkward giggling moment, I said, "I give up! What's so funny?"

Michael's chuckle finally lowered, and Genevieve's mouth stopped moving.

"It's just that…" she stifled a giggle, "Who else could we have been talking to?"

We all looked around the bus. It

was empty. After seeing Michael, the kids had scattered like flies. Stevie and I began to get up, following their lead. Garrison stood, also.

Michael and Something moved out of our way, and walked, but not before I turned back to them and said, "He's my brother, you know."

Unfortunately, that wasn't enough.

* * *

"Kids, we have something to tell you."

That's the line I was dreading to hear.

Garrison and I used to be step-siblings. We lived in the same house, liked the same food, and pretty much belonged with each other. We were best friends since we were six, when he beat up the boy who made fun of me for the lisp I had when I was younger. After that, there was no competition. He and I just *were*.

But at that moment, I didn't feel so close to him. I dropped the hand I held when my mom and stepfather announced the news.

"We're getting divorced."

Chapter Two

"HEH, THAT'S FUNNY, MOM. Really funny."

I didn't recognize that voice. It wasn't Garrison. Was it me? That's when I realized it was. Garrison had started to speak. His voice sounded different, like mine. So it was me. He forced a laugh.

"Yeah. I mean, really. For a second there, I really thought…"

"I'm sorry." That was my mom. She was looking at us, and seemed kind of… guilty. My stepfather just looked down, as if he wanted this all to end.

"Things aren't working out as well as you think they are. We've been fighting a lot, and you kids were fortunate enough to be at friends' houses while that went on." She cleared her throat, and tears pricked at her eyes. "I just… I just couldn't take it anymore. I know this is hard to believe, but I'm sorry."

I couldn't allow what she'd just said to go through my brain. They were getting…what? The only word I understood was "divorce," but it still didn't fit. Garrison and I had heard them fight at 2:30 A.M. when their shouts woke us up. We heard the screams. We heard the crashes. We just couldn't believe it.

My mom had always told me to say what I meant, and to speak my mind and tell the truth. That's what I didn't stop to think when I screamed, "I hate you!" And that was just the start.

I was on my computer, instant-messaging Garrison. For some reason, I felt better when I wrote. Even though art was his passion, he did, too.

I still can't believe it, I typed.

What's not to believe, he replied, *it's not like we didn't hear them screaming last month.*

Yeah, I guess that's true. But I don't want it to be. I just want this all to stop.

"And it will," a voice said.

I jumped. "What the... Garrison?"

My soon-to-be ex-stepbrother was sitting on my bed, his Blackberry in his hands. He let it fall onto my bed and brought my beanbag to the desk where I sat.

"It's not the end of the world, Titi. We'll live through this. They still love us, right?"

"Right," I sighed, looking away. I couldn't face him, still ashamed from my outburst.

He grabbed my face and forced me to stare into his eyes. "*Right.* There's nothing to worry about. We'll still see each other at school."

14

That's when it hit me. We wouldn't be related anymore after the divorce. Whenever people used to see us together, they'd think we were dating, not brother and sister. Whenever we hugged, that's what they'd think. That would cause so many problems...

"Tina," he whispered, "I said we'll still see each other at school."

"But it won't be the same!" I yelled, forgetting to whisper. Tears dripped down my face. I couldn't do it. I wasn't strong.

Our parents ran into the room to see what the commotion was about. I pushed through the wall they'd become, blocking my exit.

My stepfather caught my arm as I was halfway out the door, shouting, "Tina!"

I slapped his hand with my free wrist. As I glared at him, I turned and hissed at my shocked, hurt mother, "I'll be at Stevie's."

"Hey Tina," Stevie said cheerfully, not turning around, headphones on ears. With my face still red, I'd walked into Stevie's house and asked to see her.

Stevie took the headphones off and turned off her laptop, which was black and covered in educational stickers. "What are you doing here? My mom said…"

Being the good friend she is, Stevie could sense my pain after she'd turned around and noticed I still had tears on my face.

She dropped her laptop on her bed and collapsed in her rocking chair in the corner of her bedroom. With wide, innocent eyes, she calmly asked, "What's wrong?"

I didn't know where to begin. My heart raced, and blood pounded in my ears. I felt like I was hanging upside down on a rollercoaster loop, blood rushing to my head after a few minutes of torture. With a deep breath, I told her the sad, tear-jerking truth, "Garrison's not my brother, anymore."

After a long pause, Stevie didn't seem concerned like she had been before. She looked angry. At first I thought it was at me.

"What did that slimeball do to you?" she exclaimed, angrily pacing around her small room and stomping her feet loudly. We lived just below her in our apartment complex. "When I see him, I am *so* going to…"

"Stevie," I whispered, not sounding nearly as upset as I felt. I sat on the edge of her bed, my legs holding me up, for my rear wasn't totally on the bed and couldn't support my weight. I jumped higher and swung my legs, so I could sit completely on her bed, only my feet hanging off.

"Stop. It's not that…what you're thinking. I mean… me and you won't be cousins, either."

She looked at me, realizing. "You're not saying what I think you're saying, are you?"

I shook my head. "Garrison's still my best friend…but his father? His father just divorced my mom."

"No!" Stevie cried, her reaction much like mine. She cupped her head in her hands and looked ready to sob. "No, no, no, and no! We're not only good friends, but step cousins! And now my stupid uncle wants to…and yours and Garrison's dad."

I shook my head. "*Garrison's dad.* He's not mine anymore. Well, until the divorce next month, things'll be really awkward around my house until he leaves."

I didn't mention that Garrison

wouldn't live with me, either. That was too painful to say. I'd already tried to erase it from my mind, but not saying it helped a bit.

A new idea formed in my now-terrified head. My heart was pounding in my chest, making me almost topple over from the pressure. I looked at Stevie with pleading eyes. "Could I, um, could I stay with you?"

Chapter Three

STEVIE CLEARED HER THROAT. She looked at me, confused.

"You want to... stay with me?"

"Of course!" I cried, exasperated. Real tears were dripping down my face. I hated it. Why was I such a baby all of a sudden? Why couldn't I stop crying?

I looked at her glumly, terrified of what she'd say, though I was afraid of the answer: "No."

I stayed silent, waiting for her to yell at me for being such a wimp. *Are you serious*, she would say, rolling her eyes. *What do you think?*

I sighed, feeling guilty that I even thought that. Stevie was the nicest person I knew, aside from Garrison. She was a little crabby sometimes, but only jokingly, never seriously. And never to me.

"I think your family needs you right now."

That surprised me. "They do?" I said.

She nodded intensely, but her eyes seeming distant. "You're lucky. You know they love you."

My heart stopped. It seemed to be doing that a lot lately. I had forgotten about Stevie's workaholic parents. It was shocking to see her mother answer the door not dressed for work. She was at work so much I didn't even know what she worked as, let alone what she looked like. I looked up at Stevie who stared at the window. I took a deep breath and said, "I'm sorry."

Painfully, she smiled at me, rocking slowly back and forth. "Our families both kind of stink, don't they?"

I nodded, smirking. "Tell me about it."

* * *

"Garrison!" Stevie cried, waving her hands wildly. I slapped her hand down. I hadn't talked to Garrison lately, not at home or at school.

"What the heck are you doing?" I said.

Stevie lowered her arms and looked at me from over her glasses. She crossed her arms. "Tina," she said seriously, staring me down. "You need to talk to him."

To my horror, Garrison turned at the sound of her soft, squeaky voice. He looked me up and down, surprised. I guess he'd gotten used to my ignoring him. I looked to Stevie, and saw a sudden and unusual smugness on her childlike face.

"She wants to talk to you!" Stevie yelled to Garrison.

I gasped as Stevie shoved me forward. It felt like I flew a yard and when I landed. I was staring at Garrison's neck, for he was so much taller than I. He patted me on the head and said, "So now you're talking to me? I thought we were on strike."

I pouted at him. "No. I never stopped talking to you. I've been busy." I didn't look at him, though I didn't know why. He didn't deserve this.

He laughed bitterly. "This isn't my fault, you know. Mom and Dad can do whatever they like. All I care about is my sister." He poked me in the side, and I forced the meanest, coldest glare I could manage, but it didn't work.

He tilted his head to the side, frowning. "We can still talk, Tina. Whatever happens, you're still my best friend. Even if you were…let's say, a witch, like you're acting now, I'd still care about you. But you wouldn't do the same for me, would you?"

He bent down and smiled at me, then grinned at Stevie over my shoulder, who, from the corner of my eye, looked triumphant.

"No," I growled, "I would…"

"Then be nice. There's no point in getting mad at me, Titi. We're still friends, right? Wait, don't answer that." He adjusted the strap of his backpack, and seemed to be considering something. "You'll still call me, right?"

He didn't sound like he had before. He seemed sad. I looked up at him, glancing around the now empty hall.

I sighed my reply, "Right."
It was quiet after that.

He nodded slowly, and it seemed like he was assuring himself when he softly agreed, "Right."

I looked up at him, and jumped when the late bell rang, pulling me out of my trance. I sighed as he walked away extra slowly, stalling until he had to go to his first class. Stevie walked up to me, her eyes shining with pride.

"I am so awesome," she squealed,

her cheeks flushed. "You should thank me."

But I wasn't paying attention. I looked down and stared at my Converse sneakers. How had everything gotten so messed up? It seemed like just yesterday Garrison and I were as we should be. He wasn't as annoying; I wasn't as moody. I sighed again, and dragged it out longer. I sounded like someone who'd realized she was having a pop quiz in five minutes. That's how I felt then.

I hadn't noticed that Stevie was halfway down the hall. She looked at me, expectant. "Tina? You coming?"

I nodded quickly. "Sorry," I whispered, and I raced off in the other direction.

Chapter Four

"I HATE THEM SO MUCH!" I CRIED, pulling on my hair and wincing as a few strands came off. I flicked them away and watched the brown strings flutter softly to my desk, where they landed and sulked in defeat. I brushed them away. Those stray hairs reminded me of my attitude right now—sad, destroyed, defeated.

But I could not give up hope. My parents could get back together; all they had to do was try. And no, Michael and Genevieve weren't looking at Garrison whenever he walked by them. That was just my imagination. And Stevie wasn't still annoying me to cheerlead. Everything was normal. Everything was calm. My leftover hairs were in place, I still had my two legs, and my toes were still too long for my feet.

I was still me…it wasn't my fault everyone else was so crazy.

Except maybe it was. I'd cried three times in the few days before, and ever since the announcement of the divorce two weeks ago, saying that word brought pain to my stomach. Garrison had asked Genevieve to be his lab partner instead of me, so maybe I'd done something to upset him. And Mom was giving me funny looks. What were those about?

Michael sat with us at lunch now, but only talked to Garrison. He spoke at us, like we were mere fleas and Garrison was the Great Dane. I didn't know why, but he glared at me now and then, and in the halls he'd swerve to the right if I went left, and he'd look at Stevie like he was thinking, *Eh, she's okay.*

All this craziness bothered me. I picked up my notebook and opened to a new page. I brushed aside my sloppily arranged homework papers and hung my backpack over the back of my chair. With a pen, I not-so-neatly wrote: "Plans to get Garrison back."

"I don't know, Tina, doesn't this seem sort of silly? We don't know for sure Garrison's being… stolen," said Stevie.

"I'm not planning to find out," I said. It was two days after I'd realized that Garrison wasn't himself anymore. I shoved my books in my locker and looked at the small mirror I'd placed inside.

With a smile, I thought, *At least the outside of me didn't change.* Same boring brown hair, pretty green eyes, freckles, and otherwise flawless pale skin.

I took out my Winnie-the-Pooh math binder and fished out my textbook. Stevie watched this process, bored.

"Anyway," she continued, taking off her glasses and wiping them on her shirt, "Let's talk to Garrison first, like at your house, where Genevieve and Michael won't be. Then we'll know for sure." She put her glasses back on. "Okay?"

I started to walk away, irritated. "Whatever," I said, looking down the hall at Garrison, Michael, and Genevieve, who were laughing together. I turned and walked to math. What did she know? Apparently, no more than I did.

Chapter Five

WHEN I WENT HOME THAT DAY, I sat at the kitchen counter. I made myself a cup of cinnamon spice tea—my favorite, and by far most expensive brand—and let my feet dangle off the stool.

Kooky, my parrot, flew in from my bedroom and landed near my cup. He leaned toward it, as if inhaling the scent of the tea. I sighed and picked him up. He always managed to get out of his cage.

As I locked the cage door, I heard a slam. Garrison! Was he home? I ran out of my room and to our small den, where Garrison sat, feet up. I was about to tell him to remove his feet or at least lay them on some coasters when I realized who was sitting next to him. The only two people I didn't want to see.

I slowed my sprint to a jog, then a walk, as I stared at the three of them. Kooky flew in again and landed on Garrison. He swatted her away, which was unusual. Normally, he'd embrace her and try to make her say what he said, even though she never listened. I'd trained her well enough to annoy him.

Genevieve smiled warmly at me, and all I could think was, *Oh my gosh. Oh my gosh. Michael and Genevieve are in my living room. This is not happening.*

I smiled back at her weakly, and she said, "Hey Tina. I didn't know Garrison invited you."

I raised my eyebrows and picked up Kooky, who squawked in protest. "He didn't. I live here." I petted my parrot's feathers, peeking over its beak at the three of them.

It was their turn to be surprised. "You do?" asked Michael, finally looking up from the television. They were watching

31

America's Got Talent, Garrison and my favorite show. Of course.

My nervous green eyes flickered to Garrison, who pretended to be engrossed in the acne cream commercial that was on. Seconds passed. Then there was a commercial for Taylor Swift's new CD. I'd have to check that out later.

I walked up to him, and Kooky flew into the kitchen. Somehow she knew what I was going to do.

"Garrison," I said softly, trying not to sound as angry as I felt, "Why didn't you tell them we're related?"

He shrugged his shoulders, still not meeting my eyes. He crossed his long arms over his chest. "I didn't know I should've. They know now, though, don't they?"

I stared at him, shocked. My hands were shaking from hurt—or was that anger? I couldn't tell. Genevieve and Michael stared at me, expecting something, anything. Michael seemed bored, or at least that's what his body language said, though his eyes flickered from me to Garrison.

Genevieve was still sitting cross-legged, but one of her legs bounced up and down. I glared at her. How was she so pretty when she was nervous?

What happened next was a blur. All I remember was my stinging hand and the sound it made when I slapped Garrison's unsuspecting cheek and the sound that my heart made when I realized what I'd done.

"Leave," I commanded to his two new friends as I pointed to the door. "Don't bother to close it."

Genevieve and Michael looked up at me, startled. Garrison wore this same expression, his hand on his cheek. He looked up at me, and his eyes said, *What the heck just happened?*

I closed the door and locked the windows, afraid that they would come back and take my brother away. I heard the faint sound of wings fluttering, and the next thing I knew my cup of tea fell to the ground. Cinnamon tea fell at my feet. I don't know how long I stood there, my eyes wide, sneakers dripping.

I have no idea.

Chapter Six

I WALKED OUTSIDE THAT DAY, my shoes squishing on the sidewalk. It was raining, and God's tears matched my mood. I was glad He was crying with me. I looked at the growing puddles and tried to see my reflection. I finally found a good one and stopped in my tracks.

I didn't like what I saw. I seemed weak. My hair was patted down and wet, but only at the bottom. The rest was frizzy and knotted. My bangs were dripping in my eyes and looked sloppy somehow. My eyes seemed a dark gray, not green with blue specks like they usually were. My pale skin was now...eerie. I looked like one of the vampires from *Twilight*, but not from the beautiful part.

As I fought the urge to splash around in the puddle, I saw Stevie's mom's car driving by. The wheels slowed as the driver spotted me, and Stevie's mother got out and looked at me, startled.

"Gina," she said, eyeing me suspiciously. "Why are you out here? Where's your umbrella?"

"Tina," I corrected. "But you can call me Fiorentina. I was heading to your house, actually."

"Oh," she said, and she smiled. "Stephanie would love to have you. It's not every day when I can come home and be with her. Hop in. I'll drive you."

The ride with Stevie's mom was uncomfortable. Her eyes darted from me to the road, and I could tell what she was thinking—I was a lunatic, but at least someone would be with her daughter. I guess I seemed that way, walking two miles in the rain without an umbrella. Finally, after what seemed like hours, she spoke.

"I hope you don't mind me asking, but why didn't your mother or father drive you? Or you could've called…"

"My mom is, uh, kind of busy now," I said, stumbling over my words. "I guess Stevie, uh Stephanie, sorry, didn't tell you my parents are separating."

I heard a gasp, and she looked at me, real shock in her deep brown eyes. "I didn't know…I apologize. She doesn't tell me anything, anymore."

No one said anything else. But she did turn and smile sadly at me, and before that moment of silence, she said, "I guess that's the excuse for your behavior."

"Tina!" Stevie cried once we arrived at her house. My hair (not to mention everything else) was still wet, and my eyes were red and puffy from crying. I looked at myself through a skinny glass vase in her kitchen. I did look terrible.

"My mom texted me…are you okay?"

"Honestly," I replied, new tears

filling my eyes, "I don't know!"

Chapter Seven

AFTER TWO HOURS OF VENTING, having Stevie rub my hair, and her mother offering me ice cream, I was okay. No, I was more than okay. For some reason, I was filled with hope. I guess I'd just had a breakthrough.

"You can sleep over our house tonight, if that's necessary," Stevie's mother offered, smiling at me. I widened my eyes in surprise, and Stevie's smile extended from ear to ear.

"Really?" I said, raising my voice. After years of knowing Stevie, I'd never slept over her house. Her parents were never around, and my mom wouldn't let me stay there alone, even with Stevie's older brother watching us.

Stevie's mom nodded. "You'll have to call your parents first." She took my empty bowl of ice cream, put it in the sink, and walked up the stairs. When she came down, she had a black cell phone in her hand.

"It's mine. Let me know when you're done," she said.

I thanked her and smiled and Stevie, who was already smiling back. I dialed my home's number and listened to the ring.

After one ring, someone answered. "Hello?"

My eyes widened yet again at the sound of that familiar voice. It was Garrison.

"Uh, hi," I said softly. "Is Mom there?"

"Tina?!" Garrison cried, and he sounded like he was really crying. "Mom and Dad were so worried! Where are you? Are you hurt? Should we come pick you up? Where'd you go?"

I wanted to cry when I heard how scared he was, but I had no tears left. So instead, I laughed.

"I'm fine, Garrison. I'm at Stevie's. She says I can sleep over. I think it'd be better, because of…well, you know."

I heard silence on the other line. Then he spoke. "Yeah. Here's Mom."

"Tina?!" she shrieked.

I laughed and said, "This again?"

"We were so worried! Garrison says you're sleeping there. Should I bring you clothes?"

"That'd be great," I said, relieved. I was afraid she wouldn't have let me. "You'll drop them off soon?"

I turned to Stevie and gave her a thumbs-up sign, and she squealed and stuck her fist in the air. "Success!"

I turned my attention back to the phone, where Mom was saying, "I'll be there as soon as I drop Genevieve and Michael off."

I froze. The phone slipped from my grasp and landed on the floor with a thud. I

41

picked it up. It wasn't broken, thank goodness. I put it back to my ear, and with shaking hands I said, "I'm sorry?"

"I have to drop off the kids—and it was actually kind of rude of you to run away when your friends are here. Maybe you could invite Gen…"

I knew where she was going with this. "No, no, no, no, no! You're bringing me my clothes, and that's it. Goodbye."

A sigh came from the other end of the line. "But Tina…

"They aren't my friends," I whispered, hanging up on my mother. I gave Stevie the phone, collapsed face-down on her couch, and let the new tears fall.

Chapter Eight

WHEN MY MOM DROPPED OFF my clothes, she frowned at me. "I'm not happy with you," she muttered, sounding just as angry as I'd suspected.

"I didn't think you would be," I replied honestly, taking the plastic bag, my other hand tapping lightly on the wooden frame of the door. I was about to close it when Stevie's brother walked down the stairs, his feet stomping with every step.

"Hey, Mrs. Fieldman! What's up," he asked, taking his iPod out of his ears and stuffing it in his pocket. He eyed me suspiciously. I guess he hadn't seen the weak side to me yet.

"Hello, Jacob," my mother said, forcing a smile so fake even a bad actress would laugh. "It's Ms. Perry, actually. Marie Perry. I'm not 'Mrs. Fieldman' anymore."

She nodded sadly, and Jacob looked at the floor, slightly confused. I knew he knew well enough not to bring it up.

He glanced at me at said, "Oh, sorry 'bout that."

"It's okay," I said, blushing because now he knew. I didn't like so many people knowing my business. Then it wasn't mine anymore.

Stevie smiled desperately at her brother and said, "Tina's sleeping over. Go upstairs, 'kay?"

"Alrighty," he said smoothly, relieved to be away from this awkward situation. But before leaving, he nodded at my mom. "I'm sorry."

A single tear slipped from her eyes, and she wiped it away before she thought I would notice. "Thank you," she whispered.

* * *

When I arrived home the next day, my heart was pounding. I stared at the door, my hand hovering over the doorknob. Stevie's mom had dropped me off fifteen minutes earlier. I hadn't moved since.

"Ina!" I heard a squeaky, rough voice say. Kooky flew out from the open window and landed on the doorknob, a curious look in her brown eyes. She tilted her head, waiting for an answer. I smiled. Everyone always thought parrots couldn't talk, but that wasn't true. *Take that, Michael and Genevieve. Ha!*

I picked her up. "Tina. Say it with me—Tina."

"Ina. Say it with me," she squawked, and she flew back in the upstairs window, leaving me alone with the door.

My fingers brushed the knob, finally landing and tightening their grasp. With closed eyes, shaking fingers, I opened the door and waited for Garrison's warm arms to embrace me.

Chapter Nine

UNFORTUNATELY, GARRISON'S arms never reached me. He stood there, watching me angrily, forehead furrowed. His eyes were red and puffy. "It wasn't cool of you to leave, you know."

I glared at him. "Wasn't cool of you to lie."

"If they had known, they probably wouldn't have come over," Garrison said softly, looking at the ground like he actually cared about my feelings. We both didn't need to say who "they" were. We didn't need to say what he'd lied about, either. I couldn't forget.

Please, I wanted to say, *You're kidding me, right? Stupid, stupid excuse. You could have told them, idiot.*

Instead, I pushed him away and said, "I'm sorry they don't like me. You can invite them over today. I really don't care."

"I already did," he spat, watching me walk up the stairs into my room. "They're playing with Kooky. I hope you don't mind.

"Liar," I cried, walking down the steps and sprinting into the living room, worried. Thankfully, they weren't there. But neither was Kooky.

"I never said they were in there," said Garrison.

I walked up to my room again. Empty. As I was about to run screaming down the stairs and demand to know why Garrison lied, I stopped short. I peaked through the crack of his bedroom door.

"She's so cute," a deep, male voice said. A girl laughed, and then I heard a squeak.

"She's kissing me," giggled the girl. I gritted my teeth. That was it. I marched into my room and slammed the door shut, picking up my notebook and writing furiously. As my pencil ripped the lined white page, I kicked my desk.

Okay, I thought, this means war.

Chapter Ten

I NEVER THOUGHT I'D GET INTO that much trouble for doing what I did next.

My plan was simple: make Michael and Genevieve flee from my house like it was hell and they were dead souls. Easy, right?

Not so much.

I felt like an architect, making blueprints for my masterpiece. The blue paper was from my notebook, and the plans were drawn in pencil. I had thought a lot about this plan, putting off all of my math homework to do so. My hand swept across the page, and I knew I should've made it on the computer, for I typed much faster than I wrote. (Forty-seven words per minute, thank you very much.)

My phone vibrated softly and I

picked it up, dropping my pencil in the process. I leaned over in my chair to get it, the phone pressed up to my ear, making my earring dig into my neck. I adjusted into another uncomfortable position, my head under the table while I still sat on the chair. Straining my neck to search, I said, "Hello?

"Hey Tina," said a male voice. "It's me."

I picked up a paper clip, then tossed it aside. "I'm sorry, who is this?" I was a little creeped out, because this stranger knew my name and I didn't know his.

"You're father," he replied quietly, his voice almost a whisper. "You're real father."

* * *

"Ow!" I howled, scooting back in my chair, clutching my head. I dropped my cell and started jumping up and down. "Ow, ow, oww!"

"What's wrong?" Mom said, rushing inside my room, followed by Michael,

Genevieve, and a curious traitor. "Tina? You have to tell me so I can help."

"Ow!" I still wailed, for I really was thinking about crying. "My head...I bumped it!"

She looked at me curiously, then inspected for a bruise. "Bumped it? On what?"

I tried to look down sheepishly, but she pulled my head back into place. "My desk," I said, "just tell me if it's bleeding. My head, that is. Is it? Wait, don't."

"Tina," said Mom, suppressing a smile. "What made you bump your head on your desk?"

I looked up at her, waiting for that smile to fade. "The shock...Dad just called."

Garrison looked at me. "Dad? You mean your step dad?"

I struggled out of my mother's grasp, shaking my head sadly. "No, not your dad. *My* dad—the one from my birth."

I expected an awkward moment of silence, maybe a few tears from my mother. But instead, I saw anger in her chocolate brown eyes.

She swiped away her tears from her tan skin, which I didn't have. "He looks just like you," she growled, "a memory I have to deal with every day. And now he's calling?! Give me the phone," she said, letting go of me finally and taking it from the floor. "Here," she said softly, tossing me hers. "Call Stephanie. I'll talk with him."

"Tina, are you sure we should do this? Garrison's popular. Why can't other people like him?" asked Stevie.

I growled. As my mother suggested, I had called Stevie. But now I realized it was a mistake.

"Because he's my friend. Or used to be," I replied.

"You used to be nice...or semi-nice," sighed Stevie. "Why can't you be like that now? Face it. Garrison used to be the total package for a friend, brother, or even boyfriend. He was smart and patient enough to be a tutor, though he's not smart anymore for, um, dumping you. He's sort of beautiful, which is rare for a middle school boy. I mean seriously, blonde hair, tan skin, blue eyes? Total surfer. And he writes, too. Poems. How sweet it that?" she said.

I really didn't want to hear all this.

"He was also genuinely nice," Stevie continued. "Seriously nice, like you. And my mom when she's not working. You can't say that about many people, though I just did. Plus, he's admired by everyone in the school, so even if Michael and Genevieve didn't like him, someone else would have his or her paws all over him. Like I said, face it. He's great."

I thought about this for a moment. As usual, she was right. Darn it, why was she so smart? "He *is* great," I said finally. "He's worth pain and embarrassment. Which is why I'll need you with me when we make those idiots hate this family."

There was a small pause on the other end. "No. Didn't you listen to me? Don't answer that. I don't mean to be all hippie-dippie, but it's time for some peace. I'm sorry, Tina. No, Fiorentina. This time you're on your own."

I couldn't talk to her any longer. Now Michael and Genevieve had caused me the loss of two friends.

Chapter Eleven

THE FOLLOWING MORNING, I marched up to Garrison who was still half asleep. I barged into his room and demanded we talk. "What's up?" I asked, out of breath. "Why'd I lose you? And you left for Genevieve and Michael? *Michael?*"

"I just don't get it," Garrison started sleepily, "why do you hate Genevieve so much? She actually isn't that bad."

"She actually isn't...what? I'm sorry, did I hear you wrong?" I sounded as shocked as I felt. "Because for a second... it seemed you were switching sides."

"There *are* no sides!" he said.

"Oh, really? Because you were acting so chummy with Michael and his little friend that you forgot one important detail—we don't like them!"

Garrison rolled his eyes, which made

me want to hate him. What a jerk, I wanted to think. But since he was my stepbrother, I waited.

"No," Garrison said, "*you* don't like them."

"What's that supposed to mean?" I didn't sound nearly as angry as I felt.

Garrison snorted. "It's not all about you, you know."

"What?" I cried, shell-shocked. "Of course it isn't. It's about you, Garrison, don't you get it? You're my best friend, and my brother. Maybe not anymore, but one thing's never changed. I'll always love hanging out with you."

"Really," he said, his voice dripping with sarcasm. "It doesn't seem that way. By the way, Stevie and I talked. You were seriously planning to make my friends hate me? Are you out of your mind?"

"They're not your friends!" I yelled, my fists shaking with anger. I wanted to rip him apart, tear him to shreds, and burn the pieces. Instead, I took a deep breath.

"Garrison, you have to choose. Me, your *sister*, or them."

"Them."

"Ex...excuse me?" I stuttered, frustrated at Garrison yet at the same time awed. How did he choose so fast? "Why?"

"Because unlike you, *they* wouldn't make me choose. I can't believe I ever thought of you as a sister. You're nothing but a two-faced brat. Get over yourself."

I watched with a growing frown as he walked away, shaking his knotty blonde mop. He climbed into bed and turned his back to me so he faced the wall.

"Get out of my room," he muttered, and my feet moved on their own. They brought me into the hall and into my bedroom, where Kooky was asleep in her cage.

From the hall, I heard Garrison's sheet flutter. I turned, hope bubbling inside me. But all I saw was a hand reach out and slam his door shut. "Unbelievable," Garrison groaned.

I ran to my welcoming bed and covered myself in the warm, fuzzy flannel sheets. I covered my head with my pillow and forced new tears out of my eyes, even though on the inside I felt emotionless. I wanted to feel pain, but I just felt strange. I had cried out all of my tears, now wanting new ones to fall. I touched my heart and sighed into my pillow. Why was I being so mean? The sheets didn't feel so warm anymore.

Chapter Twelve

I WALKED INTO SCHOOL THE following Monday alone, my head down. I felt mopey, yet emotionless, as if what had happened just hadn't hit me yet. I walked to my locker, greeted a few of the nerds who stared at me in wonder, and got my books.

"Hey Tina!" said a cheerful voice, full of genuine sweetness.

"Hey Tiffany," I said, forcing a smile at the perky brunette. Tiffany, one of Genevieve's and Michael's old friends, had left them for a new group—the average kids, the ones who were teased sometimes.

Tiffany, in many ways, belonged to no specific group. With her glasses and braces, pretty features and a skinny body, she was a great person, a nice one to look up to. She got straight A's and was in all honors, and loved chess and was excellent at sports. She was the type of girl who everyone wanted to be, but were too scared to be because they cared about being popular.

"Uh, I was wondering…" Tiffany started, "and I know this isn't any of my business, so it's strange of me to ask this since we aren't really friends." She adjusted her glasses. "Garrison and you haven't been so close lately, and since he's been hanging out with Michael and Genevieve, I just thought…"

That was it. I couldn't take it anymore. I ran to Tiffany and hugged her, grateful her for her genuine kindness and worry. "Thank you."

I knew one thing would never change. As long as I had one friend, I could do anything.

She awkwardly hugged me back. "I'm sorry," she said quietly, looking around the hall and glaring gently at the people who looked. She pulled away. "Would you like to sit with me at lunch? I hate it when people sit alone. Really, you'll fit right in."

I smiled at her. "Thanks. I'd love to."

Just then the bell rang. Tiffany jumped and I laughed. I raised my eyebrows. I'd actually laughed. "See you later," I said cheerfully, and I walked into math. She waved to me.

"I'll help you get them back!" she called.

Chapter Thirteen

I WAS SO SHOCKED AT WHAT Tiffany had said. She was really willing to get me my friends back? I hardly knew the girl. She was so nice.

Suddenly, my mind was rewinding to when I'd met Tiffany for the first time in third grade. I wasn't the most popular kid, always teased for my height, and I was ashamed of myself. I didn't even want to live.

She stood up for me, saying to the others, "That's not nice. Just stop." I'd been best friends with her then, but then I met Garrison and Stevie and she was erased from my mind.

Of course, being the oversensitive, dramatic baby I am, the things they weren't too bad, but still pained me: "You're so short" and "You look like you're four".

Still, words hurt. I mentally pressed fast-forward to when Garrison called me a brat. Words *did* hurt. But with Tiffany's help, maybe Garrison and I could overcome them. Once Stevie saw the old me was back, I'd be okay.

Stevie. I took a deep breath and put my head on my desk in class. I'd forgotten. She sat at Tiffany's table now. I looked at my sneakers. Tiffany...what was she planning?

* * *

"Come on Tina, just sit next to me," Tiffany whispered as I nervously clutched my tray on the way to her table. She balanced her tray with one hand and kept her arm on my shoulder protectively, not that I needed it. Garrison, Michael and Genevieve couldn't hurt me anymore. We were opposite magnets.

She steered me over to a random

seat and plopped down next to me. Her friends stared at me in wonder. While Tiffany was introducing me, I took in my new school-friends, the ones I probably would never hang out with after school, but friends that were good enough.

There was a girl with brown hair sitting next me, and she constantly reminded me of her name, Starr. I thought it was very pretty. She had light blue eyes and her crazy brown curls with lime green and bright blue streaks. She had cute dimples and a friendly, mischievous smile. Her skin was tan, with only a few imperfections here and there, hardly noticeable. She was tall and well built, with small muscles on her arms and legs from ballet. She instantly struck me as interesting.

Then there was the girl across from Tiffany and me, somewhere in the middle. Her name was Angelee, and she was in all honors, like Genevieve. She was cool. She had short black hair and chocolate brown skin. Her eyes were muddy brown which looked gross on some people, but good on her. She was sort of average. Her eyes were her best feature. Angelee told me her favorite sport was soccer, and she'd been playing it since she could walk. She also loved to sing. She was very nice.

Next was Luke. He was handsome, with jet black hair and dark, dark brown eyes, almost black. He, like Angelee, was dark-skinned, and that's when I realized they were related. They had the same eyes, not the color, but the same wide, almond shape.

When I sat, he smiled at me, and my heart fluttered a little, but I ignored the feeling and turned to Tiffany, who was speaking. "That's okay with you, right, Tina?"

"Huh," I said stupidly, looking at her, the confusion clear in my eyes.

Tiffany laughed. "Stevie's sick today.

I know you and she have been fighting, but I wanted to invite you to sit with us, so I guess today is bad for Stevie and good for you. I'm going to go to the nurse's office with Starr and Angelee to call her. You'll stay here, with Luke. That's okay with you, right?"

"Um, right," I said quietly, looking through my eyelashes at Luke. He was staring at me, too, and quickly averted his eyes. I knew he thought that what he did was polite, but I wanted to see the brown in his eyes.

I pouted, then whispered to Tiffany, "Can't Starr or Angelee stay here?"

She looked confused for a moment. "No way, they want to talk to her, too. Back in a sec, okay?"

"Okay," I sighed, crossing my arms over my flat chest. "Just…hurry back."
She raised one eyebrow and said, "Sure, okay."

She walked away. That left me alone

with Luke. He was looking at me curiously. "What's going on with you and Stevie? And what about that Garrison kid?"

I looked down, then at Garrison's table where Michael was sneaking one of Garrison's cookies and he couldn't tell. When Garrison noticed, he laughed and jokingly smacked his friend's head, and Genevieve laughed and covered her mouth to hide what she was eating.

I looked back at Luke. "It's a long story."

"It's a long lunch period," he replied, putting down his plastic fork, grinning and preparing to listen.

I smiled at him, relieved that someone was going to let me vent, not just want to make me feel better. I'd been hiding it inside for too long. I twirled my plastic fork in my plastic spaghetti and began the story.

It was the beginning of a beautiful friendship.

Chapter Fourteen

"WOW," LUKE SAID FINALLY, glancing up at my face quickly. "That's…rough. Even if I wasn't a crybaby, I'd feel bad."

I laughed weakly, drained from the talking. Lunch was almost over, his friends were still chatting with Stevie, and I felt awkward with the confession. But he was a good listener. He nodded and stayed quiet, didn't open his mouth to interrupt, and he actually seemed to care.

"You're a crybaby?" I asked.

He blushed. "Sensitive guys can be brave guys."

I giggled. "You're not making any sense."

He shrugged. "Whatever." Luke looked to the side, and that's when I noticed the single tear drip down his cheek.

"I feel what you're feeling," he said softly, and I was surprised. I'd never seen a boy cry, ever.

He snorted suddenly. "I'm such a wimp," his voice cracked, "but me and Angelee? Our parents are divorced, too. My dad—I miss him a lot."

"Yes, I understand. You should be glad you have a sibling to share the pain with. And my mom and *stepdad* are divorcing. I don't even know my real dad. Did I forget to mention that?" I said. "He just called me a few days ago. I'd be fine if he called me any other time...but in the middle of all of this, I'm not so sure how much more I can handle. Now come on, we better get going. Don't want to be late for sixth period."

Luke nodded. "See you later."
I smiled, secretly thrilled there would be a later.

* * *

In class, I was embarrassed. I kept

69

thinking about Luke. I hated myself for that. My family was breaking, yet I was still amused with silly crushes. I shook my head. He shouldn't get involved with someone as emotional as I, especially at this young age of twelve. A year later, maybe. But not now.

My thoughts wandered to Garrison and Stevie for a moment. Stevie. I hadn't seen her in ages. I missed my friend. And Garrison. Every afternoon I dreaded seeing him at home. But what was worse were the times when he wasn't at home. I knew he was either with Genevieve or Michael or his stepdad looking at new houses, and that killed me.

Even though what was going on between us was awkward and painful, I didn't want him gone. He was my older brother by six months and he was supposed to be home, cheering me up, not away, bringing me down.

The bell rang, and I was relieved.

FRIENDS AGAIN

The day was almost over, and only gym was left. I took a deep breath. I had gym Mondays, Wednesdays, and Fridays. Today was Friday, thankfully. But this gym session was different. On Monday and Wednesday I'd have normal gym class—all girls with the pain of being with Genevieve. But every Friday, it'd be boys and girls. As in Garrison and Michael would also be around to tease me.

I changed into our gym uniform, bright red adult-sized tee-shirts and baggy sweatpants. I looked around, stepped out of the janitor's closet (that's where I changed because I didn't like to be seen half naked.)

I was in shock when I noticed Garrison standing there.

"You change in the *janitor's closet*?" He said, a hint of laughter in his voice. He didn't bother to hold it back. "Why?"

"None of your business," I snapped, shoving him out of my way.

He grabbed my wrist. "Actually, dear sister, it is. Now, I think I asked you a question. Why? Afraid the other girls will laugh at your cardboard chest?"

Tears pricked in my eyes, and I fought desperately to hide them. I could not let this jerk see me cry. When he was nice, maybe, but not now. I released my wrist and starting running for the gym, but Garrison grabbed me and pulled me back.

"Look, I don't know what is wrong with me today, but just stop being a baby and answer my question."

He held a firm grip on my shoulders and clutched them, and I knew I was feeling a bruise. I wasn't facing him. His eyes made holes in my back.

"I'm not answering your stupid question!" I yelled, and looked around the hall. The bell had rung already and the halls were empty. He spun me around and stared into my eyes. I found myself lost in the sea of violent waves that flooded in his blue orbs.

He looked ready to cry. "Not that dumb question. It was rhetorical. The one I asked you a few weeks ago. 'We'll still be friends, right?'"

I remembered that. A few weeks ago he'd asked, 'We'll still be friends, right?' I'd never answered. I didn't know what to say now. These past five weeks had been the most dramatic of my twelve years of existence, and part of this was Garrison's fault. But did I miss him? Yes.

I smiled at him for the first time in a month, and he was confused. I started to laugh just for the joy of laughing. "Right!"

Chapter Fifteen

"DON'T WORRY ABOUT IT," Garrison whispered, "you'll be fine." He put his hand on my back and steered me toward the school. He bounced a basketball with his free hand and forced a smile at Michael and Genevieve, who were learning to deal with me. He'd agreed to spend more time with me, but they were his friends, too.

Garrison was talking about Stevie. He and I had made up, but what about me and Stevie? I wasn't scared. I was terrified. Even with Garrison standing next to me, I couldn't do it. I knew I wasn't going to, and that killed me. I just didn't know what to say to get my best girl friend back.

"Look, there she is!" Garrison said way-too-cheerfully, pointing to Tiffany. Once Tiffany spotted us together, she widened her eyes and then smiled, flashing her braces. She raced toward us, with Angelee, Luke, and Starr at her heels.

"You made up!" she shouted, and a few heads turned to look.

Starr laughed and stepped forward. "Chill, Tiff, you're going to scare them away." Starr looked Garrison over, inspecting the boy who'd made me cry. She shook her head. "Shame."

Angelee and Luke looked at each other. "What's a shame?" Angelee asked timidly, tilting her head to the side in confusion.

Starr sighed, and dragged it out dramatically. Oh, right. She'd told me she was into theater. "It's just…we didn't get to hang out very long, and now what's-his-face is stealing Tina away…and I thought of the cutest nickname for you. Titi!"

A giggle threatened to escape my mouth, and I choked, trying to hold it in. "What's-his-face already calls me that." I grinned at Garrison, but he was too busy smiling at Starr. Hmm. They were getting along well.

"It's *Garrison,* thank you very much," Garrison said equally as dramatically as Starr had sighed. "Gosh. People these days."

Tiffany and I looked at each other. Luke and Angelee laughed, and I looked at Luke happily. Garrison followed my stare and said finally, "Another boy! Whew, I was worried."

We all erupted in giggles. Even though I had no idea what Stevie would do when she saw me laughing with Garrison and her new friends, I knew everything would be okay.

After all, even if Garrison was house-hunting, my mom and dad from birth were talking again, Kooky had been infected by Genevieve and Michael's grossness, and Stevie had abandoned me too, I knew I had my brother back.

FRIENDS AGAIN

And that was all I really needed.